JUST FRIENDS

A REAL MAN

JENIKA SNOW

JUST FRIENDS

By Jenika Snow

www.JenikaSnow.com

Jenika_Snow@Yahoo.com

Copyright © May 2019 by Jenika Snow

Photographer: Wander Aguiar

Cover Model: Woody Fox

Image provided by: Wander book club

Cover design by: Lori Jackson Design

Editor: Kasi Alexander

Content Editor/Proofreader: All Encompassing books

Just friends.

That's what I thought we were ... until we weren't, until my love for Mia was too consuming that I couldn't ignore it anymore. Until I couldn't deny it.

And when we'd lost someone close to us both—her brother, my best friend—it was that life-changing moment that I told myself to man up.

It was that loss that drew us closer, that made me realize I'd been a fool to stay back.

But we'd always been just friends.

Two words that meant a hell of a lot more than I wanted them to.

Two words that were this wall between us.

Two words that I wanted gone when I looked at her.

There was a time when I would have been fine with that title. But that time had passed.

I was done being just friends. I was ready to finally make Mia mine. I just hoped she felt the same way.

1

Pope

I tried not to be obvious and stare at her, but it was impossible. The way the swimsuit molded to her body, the toned length of her legs, the roundness of her ass. She turned around and smiled as she talked with her friends. Her breasts pressed against the suit, tapering down to her flat belly, and the sweet spot right between her legs.

I curled my hands into tight fists at my sides and breathed out slowly. I was going to hell for things I thought about where Mia was concerned.

The sister of my once best friend, she'd been in my life for as long as I could remember. She'd always just been Jonathan's annoying little sister who wanted to tag along with us everywhere. But as we grew older, I started to feel something more, something feral about Mia.

It had been the most intense desire I'd ever felt, this consuming emotion that screamed one word in my head over and over again.

Mine.

And when Jonathan passed away in a hit and run, we'd leaned on each other for support, for comfort.

That had been five years ago, Mia just fifteen years old to my seventeen.

Jonathan's death had been devastating to everyone, a blow to all of us.

But the years had passed, and had been kind to us as we all healed and moved forward in our lives.

Now here we were, both going to the same university, Mia on the swim team, me assistant coaching. I could've graduated if I were being honest, but the truth was I stayed longer extending my degree, and it was all because I wanted to stay close to Mia.

I loved her, was in love with her, but after everything that had happened, I knew being just friends was probably the best course of action.

Although thinking that really fucking put me in a sour mood.

So I made sure I was close enough to protect her, that I kept all the other guys away. And they sure as fuck came sniffing around, thinking they could have her.

If she went to the library to study, I was her study partner. If she went to a party, I was right there with her, mean-mugging every little asshole who wobbled over in a drunken state to try and get a piece of her.

If she'd told me to back off, that I was smothering her, I would've listened. I would've kept my distance, still making sure she was safe. I had to because her brother was no longer in the picture. And I knew Jonathan would want me to protect her.

That's what I told myself anyway, a huge reason I did what I did. Because I saw her as mine, and I didn't want anyone else near her.

I watched as she took her stance on the starting blocks, bent over and got into position. She was gorgeous and svelte ... perfect.

I stayed off in a corner and watched as she dove in, racing against several other swimmers. Of course she kicked their asses. Mia had a bright future ahead of her where swimming was concerned.

And wherever she went, I'd follow, because staying back and watching from the sidelines as she had a life without me in it was too fucking painful.

I was at that point where "just friends" wasn't good enough anymore.

———

Mia

I PUMPED my arms as I swam faster, turning my head and sucking in a lungful of air before doing the process all over again. I focused only on myself and not my teammates on either side of me. But I could feel his gaze on me, as if he were in the water with me and his hands were on me, holding me, guiding me.

Pope.

He'd been my brother's best friend for as long as I could remember. He'd been the person I looked up to along with my brother, as if he were family, as if he were my protector. I'd been Jonathan's little sister running around after them, tagging along. And never once did they complain.

Never once did they say I couldn't go, that I was annoying.

They'd embraced me, let me go everywhere with them. But as I grew older, I started seeing Pope as something more than Jonathan's friend, something more than an unofficial member of our family.

I saw him as something more than just my friend.

I started seeing him as the guy I wanted in my life as mine. He was smart and driven, athletic and honest. He was caring and the one person I had leaned on the most after Jonathan passed away.

And it was all of that stuff wrapped up tightly that had me falling hopelessly in love with him.

I reached the end of the pool after my laps and braced a hand on the edge, taking my other one and pulling off my goggles. I looked at the time board. Although this was just practice, I was pleased that I'd beaten the rest of the swimmers.

I looked over at Pope and could see him watching me in the corner, his arms crossed over his chest, a smirk on his face as he no doubt saw my time. He was my biggest supporter, pushing me to my limits because he knew I could do better, go harder, swim faster.

My heart was racing, but it didn't just have to do with the swim and everything to do with staring at the man I loved.

I did love him, so much that my chest hurt, the pain of not being honest with him and telling him how I felt riding me hard. I was old enough to know I wasn't getting any younger, but young enough to know I had my whole life ahead of me.

And I wanted Pope with me always.

Maybe I would've kept my mouth shut if I didn't see the way he watched me, the way his eyes always seemed to be on me. I felt his gaze like a physical touch, and I wanted more.

I craved more.

I climbed out of the pool and was immediately handed a towel by one of the aides. As I dried off, I looked over at Pope and saw him watching me.

I felt it in the beginning, but thought maybe his attention toward me was just Pope being Pope ... overly protective and stepping into the role of being a big brother because Jonathan was gone.

But as time passed, I realized it was more than that. He wanted me. I could see it in his eyes, feel it when he was near. He stayed silent, and I knew he probably always would.

He probably thought it would be disrespectful because of Jonathan. But I knew my brother would have wanted me to be happy, no matter who that was with. So I was the one who needed to step up.

I'd come to the conclusion that I was done waiting, that being friends wasn't enough. And maybe telling him the truth would ruin everything, but that was a chance I was willing to take.

Because if it meant I'd finally, possibly, get to be with Pope, I was willing to do anything.

2

_____

Pope

Genetics in Physical Anthropology was not a class I was even interested in, didn't help me advance my degree, and was more like someone speaking a foreign language to me than anything else. But I took it because Mia did and I wanted to be close to her.

By the grace of Mia helping me, I was barely passing the fucking class.

Before I even saw her, I knew she'd stepped into the classroom. It was the way my body tightened, how the air charged with electricity. The hairs on my arm stood on end and my heart started racing.

I looked over my shoulder and saw her walk inside the room, two books stacked on top of each other in one arm, her cell in the other hand.

The long fall of her dark hair was done in a braid, falling over her shoulder. How many times had I wanted to run my fingers through her strands? How many times had I thought of wrapping those locks around my hand and tilting her head back to claim her mouth?

I cleared my throat and straightened even more, feeling my pants become tight as my arousal quickened, as the blood started to pool in my dick. She looked up and glanced around, her gaze landing on mine and a smile spread across her face.

Shit, her smile could light up the fucking room.

She sat beside me just as Professor Goode cleared his throat.

"Lots of ground to cover today, everyone," he said in a booming voice.

I glanced up for only a moment, but the heat from Mia's body, the scent of lemon and cotton that clung to her, distracted me. I looked back at her to see she was looking at Professor Goode, this small smile on her face.

Instantly possessiveness slammed into me. Did

she have a thing for him? I had to admit that although he was at least a decade older than she was, he was someone who probably drew a lot of female attention because of his good looks. That put me in an even shittier mood.

But maybe she liked them older? Maybe she liked the refined, intelligent type?

All of which I was not.

"Please tell me I'm not the only one who sees it?" She looked at me then, her big blue eyes crinkled at the corners as her smile widened. "Please tell me you see how obvious Professor Goode is being?"

I felt my brows knit as I looked back at him. He was leaning against his desk, his arms crossed over his chest, his focus trained on one student. I followed his line of vision to see who he was staring at.

A girl.

I looked back at Mia and shrugged. She exhaled as if she was tired, or maybe couldn't believe I could miss whatever she was talking about.

"You honestly can't see that he is totally hard up for her?"

"What?" I looked back at the professor and the girl, glancing between them. She seemed oblivious to the fact he kept staring at her, but now that I was really paying attention, I could see that his focus was trained solely on her, his expression almost intense.

"Every day I watch him stare at her, almost glower when another guy talks to her. Kind of exciting knowing a professor wants a student, isn't it?" We looked at each other and she wagged her brows. She leaned in close. "It's like this forbidden love story."

The feel of her warm, sweet breath moving along my cheek had goosebumps forming on my arms. I curled my hand around the desk. It was auditorium seating, but Mia and I liked to sit in the very back, so there was nobody behind us to see the reaction I had toward her.

It wouldn't have made a difference anyway. I wouldn't have cared if they saw. In fact, I wanted them to know. I wanted them to see how she affected me, that I wanted her and I wouldn't let anybody come between that.

I wouldn't let anyone else have that.

I didn't respond as I just stared at her, wanting nothing more than to grip her chin with my thumb and forefinger and keep her face parallel with mine. I wanted to press my mouth to hers until she was clutching at me for support as I devoured her lips and showed her with a kiss she was mine.

In that moment, the words were on the tip of my tongue, words that would tell her what she meant to me, how I loved her. "Mia," I said softly.

"Mr. Donovan, maybe you'd like to teach the class since you have so much to say?"

Professor Goode's voice traveled up the classroom and I slowly looked at him. We stared at each other for a moment and I finally straightened, my focus on him.

He started teaching then and I heard Mia chuckle softly beside me. I glanced at her and smiled.

"Look at you," she whispered, "getting in trouble like you used to in high school."

I was full-on grinning then. "The good old days," I whispered back. She had her arm resting toward the edge of her desk, and I stared at her soft, golden skin, trailed my gaze down to her delicate wrist and long, almost fragile fingers. Her nails were painted light pink, almost a nude color. I thought about some dirty fucking things her hand could be doing in that moment.

When I glanced at her face, I expected her to be looking at me, having caught me staring at her. But she had her focus trained straight as she listened to the lecture.

God, I couldn't believe I'd lasted this long without ever saying anything to her. But I was going to change that. I was going to change all of that.

3

Pope

The only reason I'd come to this fucking party was because of Mia, because I wanted to make sure no one messed with her. I wanted to make sure no drunken asshole stumbled around with a semi-hard boner trying to get in her pants.

I'd break kneecaps before I let that happen.

I stood in the corner of the frat house and brought a bottle of water to my mouth, taking a long drink. A beer sounded good, but I had to keep a level and clear head.

Mia was across the room with a couple of her

girlfriends, red plastic cups in their hands, grins on their faces. Compared to them, Mia was low key, not done up and over the top with styled hair and a made-up face. She wasn't wearing revealing clothes where her midriff was showing or her cleavage was on full display.

Although it would be fine if she wanted to dress like that and make herself up that way, the fact that she was more down to earth, wearing a cardigan set to a frat party, and adjusting her reading glasses up the bridge of her nose, made her the hottest fucking girl to me.

I hadn't missed the handful of guys that kept checking her out, probably trying to grow a set of balls and go over there and talk to her. Hell, they could talk to the other three girls Mia was hanging out with. As long as they kept their distance from my girl there'd be no issues.

If they thought they had a chance with her...well, I wasn't above making a scene to make my point known.

But I wasn't going to be an asshole and be all up on her ass, a second skin that didn't let her do shit. She could do what she wanted, whenever she wanted. I'd just watch over her from a distance, and if need be, I'd go in and beat someone's ass to protect her.

Mia

I TRIED NOT to stare at Pope, to keep glancing over to where he stood in the corner, but he was a force of nature. His very presence filled a room. He was like an entity that commanded attention wherever he went.

There was no way to avoid his presence.

There was no way I wanted to.

"Hey, did you hear me?"

I glanced over at Rita and nodded. "Yeah, I heard you." I brought the beer to my mouth and swallowed the lie.

Rita snorted and shook her head. "You're such a bad liar," she said on a grin.

I glanced at Pope again, seeing his focus right on me. I didn't miss how Rita turned her attention to where my vision was trained. Camden and Gina were busy talking about guys ... who was a douche and who was decent in bed, and not paying attention to the fact I wasn't focused on what was going on.

Instead, I was wondering what it would feel like to have Pope's hands on me.

Rita glanced back at me and a smile spread across her face. "Oh my God," she said in a harsh whisper. "You're totally eye fucking Pope." That had Camden and Gina stopping their conversation and glancing at me.

I looked between the three of them and felt my face heat, being put on the spot. I could've lied, but they would've been able to tell, I was sure.

"Maybe we should talk about something else?" God, my face was on fire. I started guzzling the beer and the three of them laughed.

"You do realize that we see the way you two look at each other constantly, right?" Camden was the one to speak.

"Yeah, like you guys are so not subtle," Gina said on a smile.

"I've been wondering how long you guys are going to wait before you actually make a move. I've almost been tempted to make bets on who'll be the first." The three of them started laughing after Rita spoke.

I rolled my eyes, trying to act nonchalant, but I was embarrassed by the fact I'd obviously not been very obscure about my feelings toward Pope.

I could feel Pope's gaze on me and glanced over at him, seeing this intense look on his face as he not only watched me, but periodically scanned the room. I knew he was doing that to keep a watch on me, to be my personal security guard.

He'd always been like that, but he'd gotten more intense after Jonathan had passed away. I couldn't lie and say I didn't like that he was so possessive of me, that he didn't even want other guys talking to me, let alone looking at me.

"Surely you've noticed the way he looks at you?" Gina was the one to speak, her eyebrows lifted, surprise on her face.

I looked at Rita and Camden, seeing the same expression on their faces. I shrugged, feeling my face heat even further. Of course I'd seen him watching me, felt the way his gaze was a little bit more than friendly, how he seemed very proprietary toward me. But I guess in my head I'd played it off, thinking that it was just him looking out for me, Jonathan's best friend making sure I was okay.

When I glanced at Pope for what was probably the millionth time that night, my heart jumped to my throat. He looked at me with such possessiveness that I felt like fingers raced up my body. The shivers worked its way over my arms and legs, and I tried to hide it, but the way the girls were grinning at me told me I'd failed.

I finished off my beer, my throat tight and dry, everything spinning around me. For so long I hadn't been honest with him. Hell, I hadn't been honest with myself. I'd hidden my true feelings toward Pope for years, too afraid to utter them, to ruin what we had.

But maybe that feeling I got every now and then when he looked at me, when I thought maybe he felt the same desire for me … was real? Maybe Pope wanted me the same way I wanted him?

"Mia." Camden was the one to speak and I looked over at her.

I could feel Rita's and Gina's gazes on me. "You only live once, right?" Camden said. "If I had a man who looked at me the way Pope looks at you, nothing could keep me from being with him."

I was shocked a little at the seriousness from Camden. She was always the easygoing one, the flippant attitude girl in the bunch. She never acted serious about much, but right now, her face was set hard, her tone genuine.

I nodded as I looked at Pope one final time. So much time wasted. So much time lost.

This little voice in the back of my head told me

to be honest, that although it might ruin our friendship and put this awkward wedge between us, at least I'd be honest, not just to Pope, but to myself as well.

4

_____

Pope

She was quiet as we headed back to her dorm, and I was starting to get worried I'd done something wrong, or maybe someone had done something to her to put her in this forlorn mood.

But what if it was me?

Although I knew I could be a little overbearing and overprotective, maybe I was so far over the edge it had finally gotten under her skin?

She'd glanced at me constantly at the party, and although I didn't really try to hide the fact I watched her the whole time, maybe she was starting to realize that I could be too intense.

I tightened my hands on the steering wheel, this pressure settling on my shoulders. I didn't want to push her away. Maybe if she knew the truth, knew how I felt about her, she'd understand my undying need to be close to her.

I pulled to a stop in front of the dorm building and just sat there, the car idling. I looked over at her, seeing the way she worried her bottom lip. It was clear she had something on her mind, and I didn't want her to leave if she was concerned about something.

I shifted on the seat so I could face her better, giving her a moment to talk to me on her own before I pressed her. When several seconds passed and she still had yet to say anything, I cleared my throat and lifted my hand, running my palm over the back of my hair.

"Mia?"

She looked over at me, this surprised expression filtering across her face as if she'd been lost in her own thoughts, forgetting she sat right beside me.

In that moment, I realized I had to grow a set of balls and just be honest, to tell her how I felt. But maybe this wasn't the best time. If she had something on her mind and needed to unload that on me, I'd be here as her friend, not the guy who wanted to confess how madly in love he was with her.

She licked her lips and I watched her drag her little pink tongue along the full bottom one. My chest clenched, my hands itching to reach out and touch her, to bring her closer.

"Mia, tell me what's wrong." I was trying to keep my voice level, to keep the worry and need out of my tone.

But the truth was, Mia was starting to freak me the fuck out.

She shifted on the seat so she was facing me as well, her eyes a little wider, the uncertainty in her expression clear.

Mia took a deep breath and stared out the front windshield for long moments, as if trying to figure out what to tell me, how to tell me.

"Pope, there's stuff I want to tell you but I'm afraid."

My heart jumped and chills raced along my body. Instantly my need to protect her rose up. "Tell me what motherfucker hurt you and I'll kill them, Mia." I couldn't stop the animalistic growl that left me. "Was it some asshole at the party?" Panic seized me. "Mia, sweetheart, tell me."

When she looked at me again there was so much

vulnerability in her expression that it took my breath away.

"It's nothing like that, Pope," she said softly.

I felt the relief settle in me.

"It's about you. It's about me."

Fuck. Was this what I thought it was? Shit, I was getting nervous, fucking scared.

I wanted to be the first to speak, to tell her how I felt, that I was so fucking madly in love with her that I would do anything to make us a possibility.

And I was just about to say those words when she licked her lips and took a deep inhalation, which had everything in me freezing.

"Pope, it's always been you." My heart stopped for a moment.

I was slightly confused, maybe even a little hopeful. "Always been me?" Fuck, was that my voice?

She nodded slowly as she stared into my eyes. "It's always been you for me."

And just like that the world fucking stopped, life came full circle, and everything I'd ever hoped and dreamed for was right there for the taking.

I couldn't move, couldn't even stand. I probably looked like a fucking asshole for not responding. She looked so worried, her teeth nibbling at her bottom lip once more, her anxiety clear.

"I ruined everything, didn't I?" she whispered and the unshed tears in her eyes broke my fucking heart. "But I've kept my feelings for you secret for so long, afraid of ruining our friendship ... of this reaction from you." She looked down at her hands, and I followed her gaze, saw how she twisted her fingers together. "I love you, Pope. I've been in love with you for so long it's ingrained in me, a part of me." She looked back up at me and a small, sad smile covered her lips.

"Mia," I whispered.

"Even though you might not feel the same for me, I had to be honest..."

I didn't let her finish. I couldn't. I cupped her cheek, my thumb right by her mouth. I leaned across the seat and claimed her lips with mine, taking that chance, giving in. Her flavor exploded along my tongue as I licked the seam of her lips until she opened for me.

Christ.

She was soft like silk, sweet like sugar.

She gasped at first, but then moaned as she reached out and held on to me, gripped me as if her life depended on it.

"I've been wanting this for so fucking long," I whispered against her mouth and forced myself to pull back to look into her face. I saw her mouth slightly parted, her eyes closed.

She was lost in this moment, the same way I was.

I stroked my thumb along her cheek, her skin so soft under my touch. "Look at me." I was lost when she opened her eyes, the blueness so startling I found myself falling even more in love with her. "I love you, Mia. I've loved you for so fucking long." She exhaled softly, that sweet little puff of air filtering across my lips.

And then she was the one to bring her mouth to mine, kissing me with a desperation that rivaled my own. I didn't know what would happen next, but I knew in this moment, I couldn't have stopped if my life depended on it.

5

Mia

I shut my dorm room door and leaned against it, staring at Pope as he stepped inside. I'd lucked out and gotten a single room instead of having to share with a roommate, and at the moment I was very thankful for the extra privacy.

I knew what would happen tonight. I wanted it, craved it. But I'd be lying if I didn't admit how nervous I was.

He turned around to face me, his body seeming like it filled the small interior. I'd loved this man since I knew what that emotion was, since I knew he was the only one I ever wanted. He took a step toward me and my heart jumped in my chest. My throat was dry, tight. I couldn't breathe, couldn't think. Placing my hands on the cold, wooden door behind me, I braced myself, trying to act like I had my emotions in check.

He stopped a foot from me and I heard him inhale deeply. A moment of silence passed between us, where we just stared at each other.

"Look at you," he said softly, almost so softly that I didn't hear him. He reached out and brushed a strand of hair away from my cheek, his fingers moving along my skin, causing euphoria to slam into me. "How did I get so lucky to have you in my life?" He sounded like he was almost speaking to himself.

"I could ask myself the same thing." My voice was nothing but a bare whisper.

He shook his head and moved an inch closer. "No, Mia. You'll never know how much I love you, because I'll never be able to really describe it fully, never be able to show you. All I can do is be in your life and try until my last breath to make you realize that you're it for me. For me, you're my rising sun. You're the stars in the sky and the oxygen that gives me life."

I'd never heard Pope speak like this before. It was so powerful it almost broke my heart.

Then his chest was pressed to mine, his body heat seeping into me.

It felt like the world was tilting, like everything was falling right into place. Here I was, finally being with Pope, his body pressed to mine, the alcohol I'd consumed helping pave the way for my inhibitions to say "Go for it."

"You're so beautiful," he whispered. And then he leaned in even more, pressed his mouth right to mine, and gave me a kiss that made me breathless, a kiss that I'd always envisioned. Pope kissed me softly, sweetly. He wrapped his arms around me, keeping me close.

His body was hard against mine, but tender, gentle as he held me.

I knew he was holding back. But I didn't want that. I wanted to feel the raw power of Pope, the strength I knew he kept hidden, kept right below the surface. I wanted all of it.

"More," he grumbled against my lips.

He kissed me harder, adding more force. He pressed his body even harder against mine. I felt the hard dips of his muscles pressed to my softness, felt the stiff outline of his cock against my belly.

"Mia," he whispered. "Touch me. Hold me."

I lifted my arms and wrapped them around his

neck. In a matter of seconds, Pope had me lifted in his arms. I wrapped my legs around his waist on instinct.

And then he was striding to the bed, sitting down, but keeping me on top of him.

"That's it, baby," he said gruffly against my mouth.

I felt the stiff outline of his cock even more, pressed right up against my pussy. I was panting against his mouth, unable to think clearly, let alone say anything.

"Should we stop?" he asked harshly against my lips.

I shook my head. "God. No."

He broke away and looked into my eyes, his hand cupping my cheek.

"Don't stop, Pope."

He groaned and slammed his mouth down on mine. I dug my fingernails into his back, pulling him closer. I opened my mouth, and he slipped his tongue inside, stroking mine, making me ache between my thighs.

He was gently pressing his hard cock against my aching pussy, thrusting back and forth, making me want to beg for more ... so much more. He made me wish there was nothing separating us, that his erection was out and he was sliding it deep inside of me.

"I need you," I gasped against his mouth, and he pulled away. My face felt hot, my lips swollen from the blood rushing beneath the surface. "Pope."

I wanted him to take me. I wanted to feel freedom in his arms, in his bed. I wanted Pope to make up for lost time.

He didn't say anything for long moments, but I could see he was thinking hard, deeply. He still had his hand on my cheek, his thumb stroking right under my eye. My inner muscles clenched, needing something substantial, wanting to be stretched, to feel that burn.

I needed Pope.

He groaned right before he had his mouth on mine again. He fucked me with his lips and tongue, making me wish we were naked and in bed.

"You're mine," Pope said with so much intensity in his voice there was no doubt in my mind he meant it.

"Pope," I whispered.

"I can't let you go, Mia. I can't."

I shook my head. "Good. Because I don't want you to."

————

Pope

Fuck. This was reality. This was real.

My cock was hard, like a steel pipe in my pants, digging against my zipper. Every part of me was strung tight.

"I need you," she whispered.

I tore at my clothes as fast humanly possible until I was naked and she could look her fill of me. I looked into her eyes, the bright blue sucking me in, drawing me closer, deeper. I had never been fully alive until I realized my love for Mia, until I knew I couldn't live without her.

She was what being alive meant.

I didn't miss how her gaze lowered to my dick, how her eyes widened slightly … how her desire coated the air even more.

"Are you ready for me?"

"Yes, Pope," she gasped.

I held her tightly to me, kissing her until she was gasping for air, until she was clinging to me. I only stopped to tear at what little clothing she still had on and rip all the fucking material off until she was bare. So fucking perfect.

There was no way I'd deny her. I lifted her easily and just held her, wanting her on the bed, needing to see her hair fanned out over the sheets, the scent of her filling my nose, making me drunk.

I wouldn't waste any more time, not when I finally had Mia. I stood there for a moment, just holding her, staring at her, wanting to devour her. But there was no way I could control myself right here, right now. I leaned in an inch, our mouths so close that if I said one word, our lips would brush together.

"Is this really happening?"

I nodded. "It's so fucking happening," I whispered against her mouth. I set her down so I could cup her cheek. "I want forever," I said with a demanding tone in my voice. I slipped my hand behind her head, cupping her nape, keeping her close. This possessive side rose up in me like a hungry beast, refusing to be tamed where she was concerned. "I won't stop until I have you as mine forever, Mia."

I looked my fill of her. Her breasts were perfectly round, a handful ... mine. I looked lower at the junction between her thighs. Her pussy ... hell, her pussy was pink and wet. It was all for me.

"Pope." She said my name and it sounded so fucking good.

God, there was no turning back. There was no stopping this.

6

Pope

I was harder than I'd ever been in my life. My cock ached and my balls were drawn up tight. Hell, the tip of my dick was covered in pre-cum, the need to get off tightening my body. My gaze was trained right between her legs, the shadows in the room slightly obscuring the area of her I wanted to see the most. I took a step back and trailed my gaze up her flat belly, and over her round, perfect breasts. Her chest rose and fell, this thickness in the air almost suffocating.

I felt crazed.

"Bed, baby. I need you on the bed."

She obeyed right away and I stood there and

watched her, stared at her like this hungry beast unable to control myself.

"Mia," I whispered right before I reached toward her and wound my hand in her hair, pulling her forward so she was forced to brace her upper body on her elbows. "My Mia," I said to myself, yet I spoke them out loud. Our mouths were so close, yet not touching. "The things I want to do to you..." I let those words hang between us, knew I was probably scaring her, but I couldn't help myself. I couldn't stop myself.

"What kind of things?" She was tempting the beast within me.

"Filthy fucking things, Mia." I felt her warm breath brush along my lips. She was getting worked up over all of this.

God.

"Things that would make you blush a pretty pink color." The fact she wanted me to say them out loud turned me on so fucking much.

"Tell me, Pope. Show me." Her voice was this breathy little moan.

I tightened my hold on her hair, an involuntary act because I was getting strung even tighter, worked up even more. "I want to have my tongue on your cunt, your scream of completion in my ears." I closed my eyes as I pictured that. "I want to taste your cream on my tongue as you get off. I want to hold your breasts in my hands, feel how hard your nipples get as I eat your pussy out."

She was panting.

"I want to pull back after I've devoured you, look between your legs, and see how wet I got you, if you soaked the sheets."

The images slammed into my head on repeat and I felt my body start to shake. I could come just telling her this stuff. She lifted her hips and started rubbing herself on me.

Back and forth.

Back and forth.

My cock rubbed between her legs, causing shots of pain to race up and down my spine. I could have told her so much more, but if I did, I would have come all over her, covering the sheets and ending this before it really started.

"I want to feel how hot you are, how wet and silky the inside of your pussy is as you clench around my cock."

"Oh. God," she moaned and fell back on the bed, her eyes closed, her lower body still working back and forth on me.

I felt beads of sweat dot my forehead as I

strained to gather my control. "No other man will ever know what you feel like, taste like, smell like, Mia. All of that is for me only."

"Yes," she cried out. "I'm yours."

Yeah, she fucking was.

I needed to see her get off while she rubbed her pussy along my dick. I reached between us and found her clit, rubbing my finger back and forth over her, feeling how engorged the little bundle was.

"Come for me, Mia. Let me see you get off." I gripped her waist with one hand while I worked her clit over with my other one. She rocked her hips up and down, seeking that pleasure, that completion.

Her pussy ran over my cock seamlessly and I couldn't help but stare into her face, transfixed, mesmerized by the sight of her pleasure washing over her face.

This was all because she wanted me, because she loved me.

"That's it," I murmured. I was breathing so damn hard, and I felt my pulse racing. "Come for me, Mia."

And she obeyed right away.

With her head tossed back, her neck straining, and her hands on either side of her clenching the sheets, I felt my mouth part as I watched my girl come for me. It was the hottest thing I'd ever seen, the most arousing experience I'd ever had. Knowing she found pleasure because of me had me forcing myself not to come.

She reached up and held on to me, digging her nails into my forearms, giving in and holding on to me for stability.

When her body finally relaxed, only then did I pull my hand away, holding it up and looking down at my fingers. They were glossy from her cream. I sucked the digits into my mouth, licking off her essence, her arousal. I groaned at her flavor. Sweet musky. All mine.

I cupped the back of her head and pulled her up so I could kiss her, so I could make her taste herself on my tongue and lips. When I pulled back, we stared into each other's eyes. "I love you and I'm never letting you go." I slammed my mouth back down on hers, kissing her until she moaned for me, until she clung to me like her life depended on it.

"Pope," she gasped out when I pulled back. She was so worked up for me. So ready. Her pupils were dilated, her body warm, aroused.

"Tell me what you need and it's yours."

"You," she said instantly.

I lowered my gaze to her mouth, loving that her

lips were red, swollen, a light, glossy sheen covering them.

"Say it again." I lifted my hand and ran my finger over her bottom lip, pulling the flesh slightly down, growing harder by the second. "Again."

She gasped and I slid my finger into her mouth.

"You," she murmured around the digit.

I pulled my finger free from her mouth and breathed in and out harshly.

"I'm ready, Pope. I'm ready for everything."

I cupped her nape, pulled her in close, and claimed her mouth. The world tipped on its access, that small kiss taking my breath away, having me rethinking everything I knew about life.

It was perfection. It was now my reality.

I wasn't going to deny either of us any longer. I curled my body around hers, keeping her close, protecting her as much as I needed to feel her pressed against me. Her breasts pressed right to my chest, the perfect mounds having the very male side of me rise up.

"Mia," I said gruffly.

"Pope."

God, the way she said my name was like pouring gasoline on a fire. It was dangerous.

This small sound left her.

I broke the kiss, had my hands on her hips, my fingers digging into her body. I was being a little too rough, I knew that, but I couldn't have stopped myself even if I tried. I was like a derailed train in that moment.

I lowered my gaze to focus on her lips. So red and plump. I dipped my head just enough to run my tongue over first her top one and then the bottom. She moaned, and I kissed her again. My control was snapping.

"*Mia*." I breathed against her mouth, not wanting to pull away. "I want to take my time with you, but right now it's a losing battle." I pulled back and looked into her face.

"Then we both can lose, Pope, because right now all I want is you."

7

Mia

The way Pope watched me was reminiscent of how a lion watched a gazelle right before attacking. Precise. Intent. Consuming.

I felt possessed by his look alone.

"Mia." He said my name harshly, this groaned whisper leaving his lips. "I'm starving for you, so hungry I don't know if I'll ever get enough." He made this low sound deep within his chest. He had my body pressed to his, his mouth on my throat.

He used his teeth and tongue to lick and suck at me, to draw me closer to the edge of oblivion. His dick was pressed right between my thighs, this massive length that had me wondering if he'd even fit comfortably. My inner muscles clenched, my pussy becoming wetter.

"Mia. Baby. Show me where you want me to touch you. Take my hand and show me." He sounded pained as he spoke.

My entire body tingled, fire racing along my skin, igniting me, causing this inferno within me. He ground himself against my belly, his dick digging further against me.

"Show me," he said again, this harsh growl leaving his lips.

I took his hand, pushed it between our bodies, and while staring into his eyes, I placed his fingers right between my legs. That small touch had my toes curling, my throat tightening, and tiny sparks of electricity moving through me.

"That feel good?"

I nodded, my eyes closing on their own.

"I KNOW you deserve slow and easy, but Christ, Mia, I can't control myself where you're concerned."

My entire body felt like it would combust at any second. I was wet, ready, aching for him.

I was primed.

"I trust you. I want you however you want to take me." I didn't want him to think I'd break. Because the truth was, I'd been waiting for this moment forever.

He had his mouth back by my throat and ran his tongue along the arch of my neck, gently nibbling my flesh. He started gently adding pressure between my thighs, and I could have climaxed from that alone.

"I want to get lost in you, Mia." He pulled back and looked me in the eyes. "I want to get lost between your legs."

The air was violently sucked out of my lungs in that moment.

I was light-headed, the ecstasy I felt unlike anything I could have ever conjured up in my fantasies. I took a stuttering breath, trying to suck in oxygen, trying to keep my composure. I didn't want this to end before it really began.

He shifted back an inch, and my body chilled instantly.

Pope was on his knees between my legs, his cock in his hand. He stroked himself as he watched me. "You have no idea how long I've waited for this moment, how many times I jerked off to the image of you just like this."

My heart thundered painfully.

"Truth is, I could come just from staring at you, Mia."

I couldn't breathe, didn't think I could handle much more. Yet I'd never stop this.

"Mia," he commanded with a thick voice, his intention clear from the way he looked me, in the tone of his voice. Pope knew what he wanted, and that was me.

I lifted my upper body up even more so I was only an inch from him now, our chests almost touching. I inhaled deeply, my head tilted back so I could look in his face.

His focus was on my lips.

I wanted to touch him, to make him feel as good as he made me feel. I wrapped my fingers around his cock, his thickness startling. He was huge, too thick for my fingers to touch. I stared into his eyes and started stroking him gently. It was the change in his breathing that told me what I did affected him.

"God damn, Mia," he groaned gutturally.

I moved my hand faster, adding more pressure. I felt the wetness of pre-cum at the tip of his shaft with every upstroke. He closed his eyes, his massive chest rising and falling, his lips parting slightly. The fact I was the one giving him this pleasure had me on the verge of climaxing.

But before I could get him off, something I desperately wanted, he gently pushed my hand away.

He opened his eyes, his pupils dilated. "If you keep that up, Mia baby, I'll come before we even fully start." He was close enough that when he leaned in, our mouths were right by each other, our lips barely touching, his breath mingling with mine.

I sucked in a deep breath, the room thick, the pressure mounting. "Pope. I need you. Now."

"And you'll have me. Every part of me, Mia." And then he had his mouth on mine, fucking me with his lips and tongue. I held on to him, knowing that if I didn't I'd float away, the very presence of Pope my stability.

"How ready are you for me?" His words were muffled against my lips.

I felt like I'd been waiting for this my entire life. "I've never been more ready for anything."

8

Pope

The things I wanted to do to her...

"Lie back fully, Mia. Now." I should be gentle with her, but there was no fucking way I could control myself.

Stopping this, making myself move back, meant my self-control was slowly waning. I couldn't breathe, felt dizzy, insane with lust, with need.

No more fucking around. I wanted to feel Mia naked and pressed against me. I wanted to feel her quiver and hear her cry out for more. I wanted to feel her tight virgin pussy squeezing my cock. I wanted to see the way her expression changed as she came for me. I wanted to hear Mia calling out my

name when the ecstasy became just too much. I
wanted her to say she was mine, only mine, while
my big, thick cock was shoved deep inside of her.

"Mia." I groaned her name. I was barely hanging
on as it was.

I need to go slow. I have to be gentle with her.

But truth was, I didn't know if I could be. I was so
far gone in my need, I couldn't even control my
breathing, let alone my passion.

I stared at Mia as she lay on the bed, her hair
fanned out around the pillow, her creamy skin on
full display for me.

I lifted my hand and ran it over my mouth, a
deep groan being ripped from me but muffled by my
palm. "Spread for me."

I couldn't help but take in every inch of her,
every line, every perfect fucking curve. It was exactly
how I'd seen her in my head for all these years,
claiming her, making her mine.

I reached for my dick, stroking myself as I stared
at her, needing her like I needed to breathe. There
was no way I could be slow and gentle. No fucking
way. I was on top of her a second later, had my
mouth on her neck, my tongue at her pulse point.
She clung on to me like her life depended on it.

"Let me in," I murmured against her throat and

she spread her legs wider, letting me settle between them. I felt her slick folds surround my cock, and I started moving back and forth.

Shit, I could get off from this.

"Mia," I groaned and moved my mouth to hers, let my lips brush along hers as I spoke.

I closed my eyes and groaned.

"Feels so good, Pope," she cried out. Her eyes were closed, her lips parted.

I slipped my finger down her cleft, teasing her clit. And then I ran the pad of my thumb along her pussy hole. She writhed beneath me.

"God, Mia." I was between her thighs, my breath moving along the most intimate part of her. With my hands on her inner thighs, I kept her legs spread for me. I lifted my gaze and stared at her.

"I'm going to make you feel so good, baby."

"You already do. You already have."

I kept my gaze locked on hers as I dragged my tongue through her cleft. I had my hand on her belly, holding her in place as I ate her out.

I became a beast then, gripping her thighs tightly, digging my fingertips into her flesh, knowing there would be bruises in the morning. But I wanted those marks on her. It would show everyone who she belonged to.

The silky-smooth feeling of her pussy along my tongue could have had me coming right then. But no fucking way was I going to get off without being inside of her. I needed to feel her come for me.

Over and over I licked and sucked on her, knowing I'd never get enough, knowing she needed more. I wanted to have my face buried between her thighs until my tongue and lips were numb, until she was so weak from coming, until she was begging for more. I started dry humping the bed, not able to help myself, not even about to pretend like I could. Over and over I did this, rubbing my hips back and forth on the sheets.

When I felt her body tense and knew she was coming, I sucked her clit harder and rode out the orgasm with her. I gave her pussy one more swipe then felt her relax.

I moved up her body. My dick was pressed between her slick folds. I took her mouth in another hard, deep kiss, wanting my dick buried in her pussy so fucking badly I could already envision how good she'd feel, how tight she'd clench around my shaft.

She opened her mouth, and I didn't stop myself as I plunged my tongue inside, fucking her there.

She panted against my mouth and spread her legs wider. I pressed my hips farther against hers, my cock sliding right between the center of her, gathering her wetness.

"Spread wider for me, Mia. I need to see every inch of what's mine." I barely got the words out.

She made a soft sound in the back of her throat, and I leaned back, bracing my hands beside her, looking down at her pussy. And then this gruff sound left me as I stared at her cunt.

She was so fucking perfect between her legs, pink, wet ... mine.

"Pope," she whispered.

"Christ." It was all I could get out. I glanced up at her face, saw desire covering it, then immediately looked between her thighs again.

She was all for me.

"Be with me. No more waiting."

I groaned, my balls drawn up tight. I was about to come. I needed to be inside of her before I got off all over her belly. "Mia," I whispered harshly and grabbed my cock, the pleasure instantly consuming. As I stared into her eyes, I placed the tip at her entrance. "God. Yes." I inhaled, smelling her sweet scent, needing every part of her ingrained in me.

I opened my eyes and stared into her face. Her pupils dilated, her mouth parted.

"You ready for me, pretty girl?"

"I'm yours."

"You want me inside of you?"

She nodded.

A part of me wanted to prolong this, but the stronger part needed inside of her now.

In one swift move, I buried my cock in her wet, tight pussy. She gasped, her pain clear, instant. I stilled, letting her get accustomed to my size, my girth.

"I'm sorry," I grunted as her pussy muscles contracted around me.

"You're big." I saw the way her throat worked when she swallowed.

"Touch me," I demanded, pleaded.

She had her hands on my biceps, her nails pricking my skin.

I started pulling out and pushing back into her slowly, easily, letting her get used to me, to my size. But all I wanted to do was pound the fuck out of her. I felt how wet she'd become for me, heard her breathing change. She was right here with me.

In and out.

In and out.

Sweat started to coat my skin, my heart raced, and my balls were drawn up tight. I wanted to come so badly, but I didn't want this to end. I wanted it to last forever. For-fucking-ever.

I pushed in deep and stilled, feeling my muscles relax and contract. Her pussy milked me for my cum.

"Baby, I can't last," I admitted.

"Good, because neither can I."

I closed my eyes and moaned right before I started slamming in and out of her, fucking the hell out of my girl.

I reached between us, needing her to get off for me just once more, needing Mia to show me how good this felt for her.

I started rubbing her clit.

"Pope," she whispered.

Back and forth I rubbed that little bundle.

She tensed beneath me, moaning softly, her voice rising higher. And then she was tossing her head back and forth, her mouth opening as her pleasure reached its peak.

The fact she came for me, let herself become vulnerable, had my self-control slipping.

"Don't stop. Please, Pope," she moaned. "Don't ever stop."

"Never," I growled.

Any kind of self-control snapped. I started to

really pump in and out of her, filling her up with my cock, making her take every single thick inch. I stared at her face the whole time, loving the pleasure that washed across her expression.

"So good, Mia. So fucking good."

"Yes," she cried out.

I felt my orgasm rise. Just before I came inside of her, filling her up with my cum, I pulled out. I grabbed my cock and stroked my hand over my length, my balls drawn up, my need violent. There was no turning back, no stopping this. She was mine irrevocably. She always had been. She always would be.

The pleasure consumed me, controlled me. I breathed out slowly as my orgasm washed through me, claimed me. It was never-ending. It was uncontrollable.

Groaning deeply, I forced my eyes to stay open as I came so I could stare at her, watch as my cum covered her belly, marked her.

When the pleasure dimmed, I sagged and breathed out, my chest rising and falling harshly, sweat covering my body. I couldn't help but stare at Mia, thinking about what we'd done, how Mia was mine. All mine now.

Possessiveness filled me at the very knowledge

that she'd given herself to me. I felt even more territorial of her now.

I lifted my gaze to her face. For a long time we didn't speak, but nothing needed to be said.

"Pope," she whispered and my heart clenched.

"Be mine, Mia. Always."

She smiled. "I've always been yours, Pope."

Pride and pleasure slammed into me, and I couldn't help the sound of raw need that came from me. It was primal. "I couldn't let you go even if I wanted to, Mia, even if I had the strength to." I pulled her in close and buried my nose in her hair. "All I want to do is make you happy, to protect you and make sure I don't disappoint you." I felt her shake her head. "Having you in my life has changed everything. Loving you has changed everything." I wasn't like this, not ever, but with Mia I felt the world crumble around me. "You make me want to be a better person. You make me want to be a better everything."

That was the truth, but she'd never know how deep it actually ran. I'd spend the rest of my life showing her, proving to her that we were always meant to be together.

9

Pope

I started off at a slow pace on the treadmill, but the longer I was on it the more my thoughts wandered, and the faster I went. My feet hit the platform at a steady interval, the music blasting through my earbuds, sweat dripping down my body.

All I could think about was last night, what Mia and I had done ... what I'd done to her.

My body was strung tight with the memory of how she'd felt under me, how soft her skin was, how good she smelled. Even now, I swore her scent was on my skin, ingrained in my very cells.

I closed my eyes and breathed out.

She'd been so tight and wet, so ready and primed

for me. I hadn't been able to control myself like I wanted to, hadn't been able to make it last, make it go all night. And that's what I wanted.

I wanted to be buried deep inside of her until the sun had come up and both of us were too exhausted to move. But I'd forced myself to leave, because sneaking out at the ass crack of dawn from her dorm would've caused some issues for her, raised some eyebrows.

But I'd made it perfectly fucking clear that this hadn't been a one-night thing, a one-time occurrence. I meant it when I said Mia was mine and I wasn't letting her go. I'd waited too damn long to finally claim her, and now that I had her, everything felt like it was right in the world, like everything had fallen into place.

All I wanted to do was spend every waking moment with her, hold her, touch her in some way so everyone knew, had no fucking question, who she was with.

I pumped my arms faster as I ran harder, my focus trained right ahead. There were people working out on either side of me, girls in skimpy spandex outfits, ones that were mainly there to get the attention of the beefed-up guys on campus instead of actually working up a sweat.

After half an hour, I shut down the treadmill and stood there for a moment, my chest rising and falling, a sheet of sweat covering my body. I'd already been at the gym for an hour and a half, working out because it was better than the alternative, which was going right back to Mia and pressing her up against the wall as I buried myself deep in her body.

Hell, I could still feel her hands on me, her fingers gently moving up and down my arms, holding me as I thrust in and out of her. I could still feel her nails pressing into my bicep, that prick of pain as she cried out her completion.

Shit, my cock was starting to harden, my erection tenting the nylon of my shorts.

I climbed off the treadmill and grabbed a towel, wiping the sweat from my body. I picked up my water bottle and unscrewed the cap, downing the full sixteen ounces before tossing it in the recycling bin.

My chest was rising and falling in even intervals, everything around me dim compared to what I had, how I felt with Mia.

"Hey, dude. What's up?"

I glanced over when I heard Tristan's voice.

He sauntered over, the wife beater he wore stretched across his massive chest.

"Hey, man."

He stopped by me and grinned. He was a rich pretty boy, but despite his cocky manwhore-ish reputation on campus, Tristan was a good guy who was just misunderstood.

Yet I knew he liked all the attention, even if most of it was bullshit.

"Dude, big-ass party tonight over at Beta Kappa Alpha." He walked over to bench-press and turned around to look at me when I didn't answer. "You down?"

I shook my head and walked over to where my gym bag was. I sat on the bench and started taking off my running shoes. I needed to shower. And then I'd go see my girl.

"Rumor has it there's some big-time football players showing up. You played ball in high school, right?"

"That was a lifetime ago, man."

Tristan snorted and I grinned.

"You sound like you're an old fucking man."

"Compared to those days, I am." Tristan started laughing. "But I have plans tonight anyway."

Technically, I didn't have anything going on, but my plans were always Mia.

They always were and always would be.

Because she was mine.

That knowledge washed through me like a tidal wave and I felt myself grin. I could sense Tristan still staring at me, and when I glanced at him, I was right. His focus was trained right on me, this inquisitive look on his face.

"Dude, what's up with you? You look like you got a good piece of ass last night or something." He sat down but still stared at me.

I just shook my head. "Good company will do that, man." *Love will do that to you.*

And what Mia and I did was no one's business but our own. But I was feeling pretty fucking incredible, and that was obviously projecting.

"Well, your silence is pretty loud, but I'm not going to delve. I know how to mind my own fucking business." He gestured for one of the other guys to come over and spot him, then leaned back, lifting his hands and curling his fingers around the bar of the weights. "Well, if you change your mind, come on out. Supposed to be one hell of a party." He looked at me for a moment. "Maybe you can hit up some of those football players, you know, get in good with them."

I knew Tristan meant well, but he didn't know the whole story. He didn't know that after a bad knee injury that successfully ended what could have been an incredible professional football career, I decided I'd follow this new life and focus on my studies, get a job that didn't have me knocking into big motherfuckers on the daily.

Not like I had any other choice in the matter.

"But yeah, man," Tristan said on a grunt as he started lifting. "Come on out if you're up for it. Beer, tits, and ass ... all of it all up in your fucking face."

That, I did not doubt. Those frat guys liked to drink and fuck. But that's not what I was all about.

I tipped my chin in acknowledgment, grabbed my bag off the floor, and headed for the locker room. I was anxious to go to Mia, to hold her, look at her ... fucking smell the sweet aroma that always clung to her. I'd been away from her for less than a fucking day and already I was feeling withdrawal symptoms.

Shit, I was gone. I was really fucking gone for Mia. And damn did it feel good.

10

Mia

I felt the goofy grin on my face but I couldn't help it, couldn't even try and stop myself. I sat in the auditorium for one of my classes. I should have been paying attention to the lecture, but my focus was shot.

The equations on the whiteboard should have been something I'd been focusing on. I should be paying attention to it because of the test at the end of the week.

But all I kept thinking about was Pope. All I kept thinking about was how he felt on top of me, how it felt to have his hands moving over my body, his mouth at the base of my throat.

God, I was getting myself worked up in the middle of class.

I shifted on the seat, trying to calm myself down.

"Hey," Rita said from beside me and I glanced at her, giving her a tight-lipped smile.

"Hey," I said in response and hoped like hell she couldn't see how on edge I was. But the look on her face told me I wasn't hiding it very well.

"You okay? You've been acting so weird since this morning. What's up?"

I went back to chewing on the end of my pen, a nervous habit I was finding myself doing more and more these days.

"Nothing," I said and gave her another smile that was totally forced, and I knew she could definitely tell.

Thankfully she didn't press me, at least not yet.

When the lecture finally ended, I heaved a sigh of relief, realizing how unfocused I was in class. I put my books in my bag and stood, following Rita out. We both had a free block of time before our next class, so we headed out back toward the commons area known as "The Gardens," a bricked-in courtyard that really didn't have much in the way of flowers, but for whatever reason everyone called it that like it did.

We made our way to the courtyard. The few picnic tables were already taken, but the stone bench pressed against one of the far walls was free. We didn't come out here to study, mainly to bullshit about what was going on in our lives, or more accurately, what was going on in Rita's life since she was far more interesting in that department than me.

I set my bag beside the bench and sat down, leaning against the brick wall and feeling the sun on my face before closing my eyes. I felt Rita sit beside me, the scent of her perfume surrounding me instantly.

I opened my eyes and looked at her. She had her head back against the wall, her eyes closed, and her head tipped back toward the sunshine. If we'd gone to high school together, she most definitely wouldn't have talked to me. She would've been one of the popular girls. I would've hung back in the library and watched them drive off to get lunch while I ate my peanut butter sandwich between the fiction and nonfiction section.

But college was so different. The people were so different. Everyone came together. There wasn't that petty bullshit of cliques and drama. At least none I'd seen.

It was a pleasant change from high school, that was for sure.

"Are you going to tell me what's going on?" I glanced over at Rita. She still had her eyes closed and her head back, but as if she sensed me looking at her, she opened her eyes and made eye contact. "Cause I won't stop bugging you." She grinned.

I snorted. "That's the truth."

She playfully nudged me. When I didn't respond right away, when I felt my cheeks heat, I saw the way her mouth parted in an O, as if she'd read me like an open book.

"Oh my God," she said slowly, her voice low enough that only I could hear. "You finally got with Pope, didn't you?"

When I didn't say anything, but felt the smile spread across my face, her eyes widened and she looked around, as if she didn't want anyone to hear this conversation. She looked more excited than I felt.

Rita glanced back at me, her mouth still opened slightly in surprise. "I got to say, it's about damn time."

I nodded, agreeing with the sentiments completely.

"So, how was it? Incredible? Mind blowing? Soul shattering?"

I laughed softly and shook my head, but the truth was it had been all those things and more. I sobered a moment as I thought about what I felt for Pope, how what we had done wasn't just an exchange of physical gratification. We'd shared our bodies, our souls. We were one and the same, two halves of a whole.

It seemed so incredibly cliché when I thought of it like that, but if I hadn't felt it, experienced it, I wouldn't believe it was my reality.

"It was perfect, Rita," I finally said after I'd been quiet for so long. "I've wanted to be with Pope for so long, loved him for that same time. But I guess I was afraid, unsure of the repercussions of being with my brother's best friend." At the thought of Jonathan, my throat tightened.

He'd be so happy for me, I knew it. Hell, if he were still alive, he'd probably be the one to push Pope and me together. He would've seen how much we cared for each other, told us we were stupid for trying to fight it.

I rested my head back on the brick wall and listened to Rita talk about how happy she was for me, how excited she was that we'd finally gotten together. Although I listened to her, the truth was I was lost in my own little world, my fairy tale.

I'd finally gotten my happily ever after.

—————

Pope

I LAID a blanket on the ground, helped Mia down, and then took my place beside her. For ten minutes we just lay there, staring up at the stars, listening to the sounds of the night around us.

Crickets chirping. An owl hooting. There was the occasional sound of the leaves rustling as the wind picked up, of a car driving in the distance. It was a reminder that there was a world right outside of our little bubble.

It was perfection, and all I kept thinking was how I was the luckiest bastard in the world to finally have the one woman I loved in my arms, and my life. I knew she'd always be mine, and that was now my reality.

I wasn't worried about what people might say, how their confusion might be twisted into judgment. I'd been in her life for so long that I was seen as family to them, but it made no difference. I loved her and she loved me. We could face anything together as long as we were at each other's sides.

"I don't think I've ever seen the sky this clear before, the stars this bright." Her voice was soft.

I had my arm around her shoulder so she was slightly propped up, her body turned a little bit toward me and her hand resting on my waist. The ground was hard and uncomfortable, but having Mia pressed up against me, all I felt was happiness, pleasure. I could've been lying on fucking knives and I wouldn't have felt a damn thing but her body pressed against mine.

"What are you thinking about?" I said softly, wanting nothing more than to hear her voice, that melodic tone that calmed me but also inflamed me all in the same breath.

She was silent for a moment, the tips of her fingers running over the edge of my T-shirt, lightly moving against the small swatch of skin exposed from the material riding up.

"I'm just thinking about how much time we've wasted, and how I'm glad that we finally found our way to each other."

I tightened my arm around her shoulders and brought Mia impossibly closer. "Me too, baby. Me too." I stared at the stars, wondering how Jonathan would feel if he were here, if he'd approve of me being with Mia.

"I know he would."

I shifted so I could look at her. I hadn't realized I'd said those words out loud.

"I think he'd be happy for us, that he'd want us both to be happy, especially if that meant being with each other."

"Yeah, I think he'd be happy for us too."

We sat there for another twenty minutes, neither of us speaking, but nothing needed to be said. The silence was comforting.

I could've stayed there forever, just holding her, remembering all the times we'd been together, the lost moments where I could've told her how I felt, held her just like this. But I couldn't go in the past. I could only focus on the future, and that was making sure I made Mia happy, that she never wanted for anything, and that I never took this for granted.

And I never would.

She was right; we'd wasted too much time already. But we had all the time in the world.

We had forever.

Together.

EPILOGUE

Pope

Five years later

I opened the front door, immediately tossed my keys into the little ceramic bowl on the entryway table, and realized I heard ... nothing.

Not the sound of Mia in the kitchen, not the sounds of Dina running around. I didn't even hear the click and clack of dog nails from Ruby as she hauled ass toward me.

I closed the front door and just stood there for a moment listening.

"Mia? Dina?" Usually when I got home from work, Mia was close by and our three-year-old daughter, Dina, came rushing toward me to give me the biggest bear hug imaginable.

But no one was around.

As panic started to settle in, the protective instinct in me rose up. I first checked the kitchen. Then I checked the living room. I hauled ass upstairs but didn't see anyone there. Only place left to look was the backyard.

The closer I got to the deck door, the more relief settled in when I heard Dina laughing and Ruby barking playfully. I opened the door and stepped outside, the sound of sizzling meat on the grill, the scent of it cooking, surrounding me.

Mia sat on a lounge chair with her legs kicked up, her feet crossed at the ankles, and her little red painted toes moving back and forth as she hummed softly to whatever she was listening to through her earbuds. But I could see one wasn't in, a motherly act she did so that she could hear Dina.

For a moment, I just stood there and watched her, happiness settling in me, contentment filling every inch of my body. The neighbors had the sprinkler going, the rhythmic sound telling me summer had come full force.

"Daddy," Dina said and ran up to me, her little

arms and legs pumping as she scaled the steps of the deck and launched herself in my arms.

Ruby was right behind, Dina's unofficial protector, always following her no matter where she was.

I picked my little girl up in my arms and looked over at Mia, seeing her look over at me with a big grin on her face, the oversize sunglasses making her look like Jackie O. Her dark hair was piled up in a bun on top of her head, the little tank top she wore accentuating the womanly curves of her body.

Dina squirmed to get down and I set her on her feet, watching as she ran back over to the swing set. I watched her for a second before I walked over to my wife and picked her up off the lounge chair, holding her close and burying my face in the crook of her neck.

She smelled sweet, that lemony, cotton scent that drove me absolutely fucking insane.

"I was worried when you guys didn't greet me at the front door," I said, having gotten used to the welcome home reception since before Dina was even born, from the time we first bought our house.

"I'm sorry. Dina was screaming to go outside since this is the first nice weather we've had." She pulled back and tipped her head to look at me, a smile on her face, my reflection in her sunglasses.

Mia and I had gotten married just a year after we'd become official. I'd sure as fuck wanted to do it sooner, but finishing school first was important to her, and what she wanted was important to me. Then Dina came along and the rest was perfect, happy history.

"The truth was, I wanted to do something real special for tonight."

I leaned in and kissed her on the lips softly. "Yeah?" I murmured, feeling my arousal rise.

"Yeah," she said and grinned, and I felt the tilt of her lips against mine.

"What did you have in mind?"

She pulled off her sunglasses and the way the sun hit her face had her eyes looking like the lightest blue I'd ever seen.

"It isn't that kind of surprise," she said and chuckled. She took a step back and I reluctantly let her, my arms falling back to my sides as I lifted a brow.

My curiosity rose as I watched her reach into the front pocket of her shorts and pull out a little white stick, the pink cap on it catching the light momentarily. My heart jumped to my throat when I realized what I was looking at. I actually lifted my hand to place it over my chest.

"Is that..."

She nodded before I could finish. She handed it over and I took the little stick, my hands shaky as I looked down at it. Even with the glare from the sun, I could read a little digital screen perfectly.

Pregnant.

My knees about gave out, my big body leaning against the railing of the deck. "Mia, baby," I said, my throat tight with emotion. I glanced up at her and saw she had her hands covering her mouth, the corners of her eyes crinkled. I knew she was smiling. "Another baby?"

She nodded again and came over to me instantly, rising on her toes and wrapping her arms around my neck. She looked down at the pregnancy test. We'd been trying for the past year, and if I were being honest, I was starting to worry that there were issues, especially since she'd gotten pregnant so fast with Dina.

"Another baby," I said and felt my grin spread. I probably looked like a fool but I didn't fucking care. I wrapped my arms around her and pulled Mia in close. Dina came running up the deck steps, Ruby right behind her.

"Daddy, Daddy," she shouted and jumped up and down in front of me. She grabbed the test out of my hand and looked down at it with curiosity written on her face. "What is this?" Her little voice was curious.

"That just told us you're going to be a big sister, baby girl," I said and picked Dina up. I held her with one hand and had my other arm wrapped around Mia, both of my girls close.

While Dina squealed about being a big sister, telling us what she wanted the baby to be named, and demanding it was a little boy, all I could do was think whoever was watching over us had blessed the hell out of me.

I was one lucky bastard to have this kind of life.

The End

ABOUT THE AUTHOR

Want to read more by Jenika Snow? Find all her titles here:

http://jenikasnow.com/bookshelf/

Find the author at:

Newsletter: http://bit.ly/2dkihXD

www.JenikaSnow.com
Jenika_Snow@yahoo.com

Made in the USA
Columbia, SC
08 May 2019